The Fabulous Fanshaws

By

Michael Rosenberg

Illustrations by Kalpart

Strategic Book Publishing and Rights Co.

Strategic Book Publishing and Rights Co., LLC
USA | Singapore
www.sbpra.com

For information about special discounts for bulk purchases, please contact Strategic Book Publishing and Rights Co., LLC. Special Sales, at bookorder@sbpra.net.

ISBN: 978-1-68181-719-4

PART ONE

CHAPTER ONE
THE FANSHAWS HAVE A SURPRISE

Sir Waldron de Montaigne Lancelot Rodriguez Fanshaw was a very grand person indeed, or at least he thought so. With a name like that it must be true. He was of medium height but with a good noble rotund body, a rather ruddy complexion, and a very large but drooping moustache, above which sat an aristocratic nose, as he called it. Actually it was a rather red and large addition to the chubby cheeks around it, mostly encouraged by ample quantities of gin and tonic. He could trace his ancestors back through the centuries, and his many names provided evidence of those past glorious days. He should have been living in a grand seventeenth century castle in Cornwall, surrounded by acres of countryside, and served by humble staff who were ever grateful for his generosity once a year on special occasions.

Unfortunately, due to the fact that most of his ancestors regularly went off to war and promptly died in defence of their various countries, leaving their wives to protect their dwindling fortunes and estates, plus the more than frequent adventures into money-making schemes that always appeared to be fool proof but invariably ended up in disaster, the current Knight of the Realm lived in a semi-detached council house in Clapham. His wife, Lady Gertrude, had met him on holiday in Torremolinos, Spain, where she had been a waitress in the local fish and chip shop. However our Knight preferred to tell those who enquired about her background that she was, of course, descended from the Spanish line of some of his ancestors and had worked hard to perfect her South London accent in order to blend into the community. They had two children, now aged 13 and 15, a boy and a girl named Rupert and Geraldine.

Sir Waldron worked as a petrol pump attendant at the local garage where he was known as Walter Fanshaw. His wife was a check-out assistant at the local supermarket. Walter was convinced that he soon would be able to recoup the family fortunes with an amazing scheme and spent most of the day dreaming of ways to achieve this delightful goal. He also dreamed of being a knight in shining armour leading his armies to battle.

It was a rather cloudy and dismal wet day. Walter was at the garage and, trying to be helpful, he started to clean the windscreen of a car that had just been filled with petrol. As he leaned across the windscreen, he looked at the face of the driver, which was a bit weird. The driver had very pointed ears and a bald head. But what was more extraordinary, were the eyes, which kept changing colour as he looked at them. First green, then blue, then orange, and even yellow. They changed colour like traffic lights, and as he stared, the eyes stared back. All of a sudden, he felt as though an electric current had surged through his body. It was not painful but very

strange, and he felt himself shaking so much that he dropped the cloth he was using and simply stood back from the car. Another surge of electricity coursed through him. Before he could gather his senses, the car started and slowly drew away from him.

Meanwhile, at exactly the same time, which was 2.45 in the afternoon, Gertrude was at her check-out desk swiping the purchases as usual when she looked up to greet the next customer, a quite good looking but elderly lady. She was well dressed but, in the next moment, she completely changed and became an old hag with pointed ears and no hair. As Gertrude stared in astonishment, the woman's eyes flashed and changed colour from green to orange and then yellow, followed by a flashing red before returning to blue. At the same time, Gertrude also felt the surge of electricity through her body and, in her state, she found herself swiping a box of cornflakes time after time. The whole experience only lasted about a minute or less but it seemed an age. Then the old hag turned back to the smiling elderly lady who said how kind Gertrude had been and moved on and out of sight. It was 2.45 pm when this happened.

Again, at exactly the same time, Geraldine was in a pottery class at school. Miss Tamaris was moving around the class checking on their work. Geraldine was making a vase on the turntable and stroking it into shape. She wanted it to be a present for her mother. As she looked up, Miss Tamaris suddenly changed into a bald-headed, pointy-eared old hag, and her eyes changed colours, just as the others had done to her parents, though of course she did not know that at the time. Then came the electric surge. Again, after a minute or less, the apparition reverted to the nice Miss Tamaris. Geraldine thought she must have been day dreaming.

In another classroom, Rupert was in a woodworking class, and the exact same thing happened to him at exactly the same time, only this time it was his male teacher, Mr. Minton.

That evening, as the family sat round the dinner table, everyone was very quiet. No one wanted to admit to having had these strange experiences, and of course they had no idea that each had experienced the same event at the same time. After a short while, Rupert decided to venture forward and told his parents about what had happened to him. To his complete surprise, the others all gasped with astonishment and started talking at the same time, each relating what had been experienced. It all seemed impossible, but yet it had happened, and they had no idea what it meant.

When all had calmed down, they sat quietly for a moment, but after a few moments the lights started to flicker on and off and little flashes of blue light began jumping from each of them, creating an eerie glow in the room. The blue streams of light rippled around the table where they were sitting, and pools of blue light settled in the centre, growing by the second, and twirling around on the table, becoming taller and larger all the time. A dull booming sound filled the room and everything started to vibrate. The blue light began to take the shape of a body. Soon it was clearly that of a bald-headed and pointy-eared man with a strange crooked mouth and long spindly legs and arms.

The table and chairs, with the family still seated, started to move and, slowly at first, began to revolve in a slow circle, and all the while the blue creature stared at them with eyes changing colours. Then the revolving picked up speed and, like a ride at an amusement park, revolved faster and faster.

With a great whooshing sound, the family found themselves whisked into a kind of bubble which soared upwards and through the ceiling and roof of their house, as if there were no walls or anything in the way. Upwards, twisting and turning, with a strange musical but very deep sound, this strange bubble gathered speed and shot far into space carrying its bewildered and very frightened passengers with it.

Soon they were in darkest space and around them were myriads of stars. Then they seemed to enter a vast tunnel of light, which sped them even faster, deeper and deeper. Eventually they emerged and saw in front of them a huge planet which looked very like their own Earth, except it seemed much bigger. The bubble sped them towards this new world and, in a microsecond, surged them into the atmosphere and through clouds that were coloured green and red. Down below lay some beautiful fields and mountains with villages dotted around, but on the side of one of the mountains was something quite amazing. It was exactly like one of the castles in which Walter's ancestors had once lived—large stone walls, a moat around the castle with a drawbridge across, and huge towering turrets at each side of the castle.

In an instant the bubble flew through one of the walls and landed in an enormous banquet room with a large fire burning at one end and many trestle-type wooden tables, around which sat many people all dressed as though they were in sixteenth century England. There were men in light chain-mail armour suits with swords at their sides, women dressed in glamorous clothes, and dogs and other animals running loose around the floor. Some musicians were playing lutes and drums, and some of the people were dancing in an old-fashioned style. Men were dancing in lines and women in other lines.

The odd thing was that nobody seemed in the slightest bit surprised to see Walter and his family emerge from the bubble. Even more strange was that, as they emerged, they also were dressed in the same style as everyone else. Walter looked very grand indeed with his suit of gleaming chain mail armour and helmet at his side. They saw an empty table at the top of the hall with a wonderful array of food laden on top of it. It seemed natural to just sit down and join in the fun. So they did just that. However, everything was not as natural as it seemed at first glance. Looking closer at the people, Walter saw that they all had those funny pointed ears and both men and women had eyes that flashed in different colours.

The servants offering food and drink were the same. Some had different coloured skin as well—green, purple, and orange seemed to be the main ones.

Suddenly a trumpet sounded, and everyone stopped eating and dancing and the whole place became very quiet. The huge wooden door at the end of the hall opened, and three large Knights in shining armour strode into the room and began to slowly march towards Walter and his family, staring deeply into their eyes with those multi-coloured flashes. The middle Knight then spoke in a booming, but rather quaint old-fashioned style. Walter was very surprised and quite impressed to be addressed as Sir Waldron, since nobody had ever called him that before, even though it was his proper title.

"Sir Waldron, we bring news of some troubles and disturbances at the edge of your domain. Armies of our enemies are even now gathering to attack, and we need you to gather our troops and prepare to defend the castle and surrounding villages."

Lady Gertrude was more than a little worried about all these events. However, Rupert and Geraldine were very excited by it all. Rupert was too young to fight in the battle, but he begged his father to allow him to help, maybe with the supplies for the soldiers.

Sir Waldron now realised that he was expected to command and lead the soldiers into battle. Actually, on the one hand, he was very proud and stimulated by the idea, but at the same time completely terrified. He was not even sure he knew how to hold his sword, let alone use it in battle. He stood up, looking as much in control as he could. As he did so, his hand seemed to automatically reach for his sword and draw it from its scabbard. He held it aloft and swung it in the air as though he had been doing this all his life. The sword gleamed gold and silver in the light, and he shouted to the hall that he would lead them to victory and drive the enemies from the land. The whole room erupted in cheers and all the men raised their swords in unison.

Sir Waldron said goodbye to Gertrude and led the men outside. Rupert joined the many helpers at the back of the assembled army. Then things started to become very weird indeed.

14

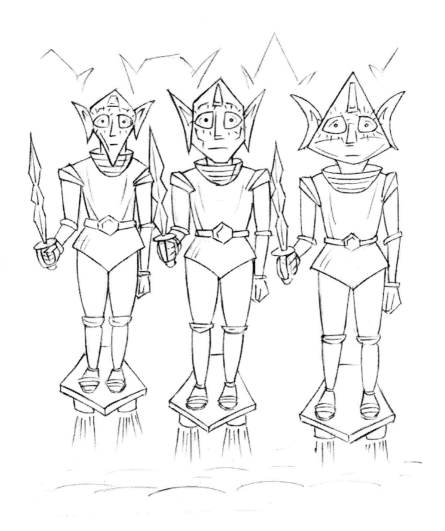

Walter, or Sir Waldron as he was now known, looked more closely at his army. He saw that they all had these funny pointed ears and flashy eyes, but also most were standing on what looked like skate boards, except that these boards were hovering about a half meter from the ground. Some had horses, but these were no ordinary horses—they had wings and also were hovering above the ground. The lances and swords carried by the troops were multi-coloured and seemed to extend and shrink from long to short at a flick of the wrist. Sir Waldron's own sword did the same and, after a little practice, he could control it very well.

At that moment a figure glided on a skate board alongside him. It was none other than the man he had first seen when cleaning the windscreen of the car at the beginning of this strange adventure. He spoke in a kind of sing-song voice. "While you were cleaning my windscreen, you were thinking very hard about your ancestors and how good it would be to experience the many adventures they had embarked upon. Your thoughts reached us, and we wanted to see how you humans would manage in a different world, so we decided to bring you into our world and let you find out yourself. My job is to observe you but also to protect you and your family. I must warn you that danger lies ahead, and I may not succeed in saving you, even though I will try."

CHAPTER TWO
PREPARING FOR BATTLE

Sir Waldron was now seated on a very large winged horse, which also had flashing eyes. He found that he could manage quite well on this animal, even though he had never ridden a horse before. He wondered if he should have a seat belt actually!!

The horse glided to the front of the soldiers. Sir Waldron lifted his sword above his head and shouted, "Follow me to victory!" A huge shout came from the soldiers and the army surged forward. As they passed through villages, the people came out to wave and cheer them on and offered food and more supplies to the soldiers and their helpers.

At first the landscape was quite flat, and they made good progress, but soon it became hilly and ahead lay some dark and rather threatening mountains, some of which were volcanoes spitting fire and ash from their summits. As they approached the mountains, the sky grew dark and swirling clouds rushed menacingly around and above the soldiers.

As it was getting late, Walter decided the time had come to camp for the night and get some rest before the inevitable difficult and dangerous day ahead of them. So they chose a sheltered place hidden amongst trees and pitched their tents. Guards were placed all around the perimeter of the camp. As they settled down to try to sleep, the forest around them was very still and quiet. However, a kind of sighing and whooshing sound gradually began to disturb them and then waxed and waned in its intensity. Mixed in with the eerie sounds was a drum beat which vibrated the very ground on which they slept. It started with a single drum beat, but grew in intensity until it sounded as though the whole forest was alive with the beating of a thousand drums.

Walter crawled out of his tent and looked around him. Other soldiers were doing the same, since no one could possibly sleep with those sounds, which seemed to fill his head with pounding noise. He looked up at the sky and saw that it glowed purple and red, even though it was the middle of the night. The colours pulsated with the rhythm of the drums, and the pitch expanded from a low rumble to something much higher and terrifying. Then a voice rose above the searing sounds and everyone heard it say: "You have no chance tomorrow. We are invincible and determined to destroy you and conquer your lands and villages. After tomorrow you will all be our slaves, if you have not perished in the battle to come."

Everyone was very afraid to hear this. Some soldiers even ran off into the forest. Walter knew he had to do something, even though he was not exactly calm himself. So, with a great voice, he shouted into the forest trying to make himself heard above the noise.

"I am Sir Waldron de Montaigne Lancelot Rodriguez Fanshaw, and I have been sent here to rid this planet of evil people such as you. We Fanshaws have fought battles throughout history in the name of good and fairness. We do not enslave people. We believe that all people have an equal right to exist side by side in peace. Each man has a choice as to how he earns his living and no one has the right to be his master. So beware tomorrow. We intend to show you our strength and bring you to your knees."

To his amazement, the noise suddenly abated and the forest became still and quiet. The clouds in the sky changed from angry reds and purples to soft greens and yellows. A few night birds started to sing in a happy kind of way. Even the branches of the trees seemed to be waving in unison with the bird song. The camp gave a huge cheer, and everyone returned to their tents. Sleep came quickly to all of them until dawn broke to herald the start of an extraordinary day.

CHAPTER THREE

THE BATTLE

As the sun rose over the mountains, the army assembled and Walter rode out in front on his hovering horse. Again he raised his golden sword and the sun reflected golden flashes from it. With a great shout, they moved forward towards the nearest mountain. Negotiating the narrow paths was the first challenge. Even though most mem were hovering on their boards, it was still risky. On one side of them were sheer drops which seemed to descend for ever. On a few occasions some of the supplies slipped from the wagons and disappeared into the dark vortex below. They continued round and round and further up the mountain with amazing vistas of the countryside stretching for miles below them. Then ahead was an even higher range, and the swirling mists began to descend around them, covering them with a kind of clammy, dewy substance. Through the mists and just above their heads strange creatures— some even had two heads—flew around them emitting weird and mournful sounds. From time to time, some would swoop down and try to steal provisions from the wagons.

It was only then that Walter realized that about half the army were robots controlled by their individual handlers. Each person in the army had, in effect, a clone of himself or herself and was manipulated simply by thought beams. Walter was the only one who did not to have a clone, at least not for the time being

Meanwhile, back at the castle Lady Gertrude was beside herself with worry and was extremely confused by all that was

happening around her. Other ladies were fussing about her and doing their best to calm her down. To keep herself busy she began to dust and try to clean the tables on which they had so recently enjoyed a marvellous feast. As she did so, the table vibrated and began to glow until she realized that she was looking at the scene that Walter was experiencing. It was, in fact, a kind of TV screen, but it was a hologram in miniature of the army, and every detail was amazingly clear with sound as well as vision.

Walter had no idea how all this was going to unfold, and just as he was thinking that it would all end badly, he felt the same surge of electricity race through his body that had started this whole thing back in Clapham. At the same time, a figure appeared next to him or, to be more precise, *hovered* next to him. It was the same creature with flashing eyes, and he simply raised his arms. As he did so, it was a though a great flowing cloak enveloped

Walter, but this cloak was something very special. At first it simply covered him from head to toe in its shiny golden folds, but then it lifted him into the air so that he was hovering above his army. What was even more astonishing was that he was expanding and getting bigger by the minute. Soon he was over ten feet tall and found that he could swoop through the air and dip and dive just like a gigantic swallow. It was an amazing feeling, and it took him quite a few minutes to accustom himself to this new world where he was able to perform incredible tricks in the air. He tried a small summersault first and felt a bit dizzy, but then as he mastered the environment, he began to enjoy the whole experience. Soon he was able to control his flight and realized that he now had a good chance to win the day so long as he was careful and cunning.

As Walter hovered above his army, his flying cloak surrounding him gave off a golden glow from the rays of the sun. At the same time, he found that his voice was magnified many times so that he could address his troops easily. They all lifted their weapons high above them and whooped with delight to see their leader looking so powerful.

Just then, swirling mists arrived and blotted out the view ahead of them for a moment. When the mists cleared, they saw stretched out in the near distance the enemy army, all looking fierce. There was a variety of soldiers, all coated in armour, some on foot and some seated on rather strange animals. Some could fly and others appeared to have two sets of arms, all carrying weapons. Seated on a huge dragon-like creature was their leader. He was dressed in a massive black cloak and had horns that gleamed in the sunlight. The dragon had vast nostrils from which poured steam and fire. It was a very frightening sight.

Walter, however, was an equally frightening sight. He was super confident that with his magical powers he could deal with almost anything that came his way. This Walter was a different person from the car window cleaner from Clapham.

Just then a figure appeared beside him. To his surprise it was his son, Rupert. "Dad, I know I am young, but right now I want to be at your side and share in the victory which I know we will achieve. I want you to be proud of me as I show you what makes a Fanshaw special." Rupert also had a great cloak and was astride a white unicorn. He too had grown in size and was clad in silver armour. Walter was indeed very proud of his son.

Together they raced with their troops towards the enemy. At the last minute Rupert swerved to the left and Walter to the right so that the enemy was confused. Then, from both sides, they let fly a hail of arrows and other deadly missiles, which divided several times as they approached their target, spraying the enemy with a gas that caused them to fall to the ground. Then Walter and Rupert swooped back together over the enemy and, along with their troops, landed among the confused creatures. They saw the enemy leader standing next to his useless dragon, who had been immobilised by the gas. Now he was begging for mercy.

One blow with his sword would have finished him off, but Walter came from a long line of chivalrous knights. He simply could not be as wicked as his enemy would have been. So, with Rupert by his side, he simply asked the enemy leader for his oath and solemn promise to leave this land and never return and to recognise the Fanshaws, and all the Fanshaws who followed, as his masters for all eternity. There was a very long pause before he received the answer he demanded. Even the dragon, who had now woken up, bowed his head in agreement.

Gertrude was watching all this from the castle and whooped with delight. Geraldine was with the other helpers at the back of the army and rushed forward to greet her dad and brother. She was so proud of them. Her smile lit up her whole face.

The victorious army marched and flew back to the castle, being welcomed along the way by cheering and happy villagers, who had been hiding and now were overjoyed that the battle had been won. A huge feast and party was being prepared for their arrival.

CHAPTER FOUR
BACK AT THE CASTLE

It was strange for Walter to experience the combination of medieval surroundings mixed with hi tech sounds and lighting effects. In the castle were wooden tables laden with all kinds of exotic fruits and meats and glasses full of the most delightful drinks in a multitude of colours. They were served by robotic wait-staff, all humanoid in character. The room vibrated and pulsed to the rhythm of an amazing band of musicians playing the strangest instruments they had ever seen, as the walls changed colours, matching the mood of the music and the intensity of the sound.

From time to time holographic images would appear showing scenes of the recent battle. Every time these appeared, a great shout filled the hall.

Then a voice interrupted Walter's enjoyment. It was the fiery eyed creature again. "Now you have another test of your character. We may appear most advanced in some ways with all kinds of technology, but our children are becoming lazy. All they have to do is to press a button or speak to a robot and anything they want to know or do is automatically arranged. We are very worried that soon we will be ruled by those robots and, in effect, become slaves, just as your ancestors owned slaves. You probably do not realise that the army you defeated was mostly made up of robots, so it was an important victory. It is really important that we find a way to prevent another disaster happening."

Then Walter felt he had to ask a question. "What is your name?"

The creature responded with, "I am known by many names, but you may call me Cantrans."

Walter gathered his family around him. They wondered why he looked so serious when everyone was having such an enjoyable time. After they had listened to him, they realised that something needed to be done to help these people. It was Geraldine who came up with the obvious idea. "We need to set up a special school to teach the basic knowledge that we are used to back on planet Earth. Computers and robots are all useful, but people need to relearn how to think for themselves. Mum, Rupert and I would love to help. At least two hours every day should be devoted to studying a mixture of English and maths, so the children learn how to write and appreciate good literature and use their brains to work out problems without relying on machines to help them. Of course they also would learn the new technologies, but it is important that they appreciate art and drama and learn to be creative and use their imagination, in addition to the amazing new science surrounding them."

Walter was very impressed by this idea coming from his daughter and, with the help of some of his new friends, he began to organise a special room in the castle and make arrangements to begin this new enterprise.

The first class was a very strange affair. About twenty children, ranging in age from eight to fifteen, came to the classroom. It was clear they had come under protest. Many had brought their robot friends and their hover boards as well as the gadgets they were used to, such as smart watches that had the ability to project holographic images and special pens that could write without being touched. The only way to deal with the students was to be very strict.

Gertrude made it quite clear that she was in charge and would stand for no nonsense. They decided to split the group into three sections by age. Geraldine and Rupert each took a group of younger ones and Gertrude took the group of older ones. All were told to hand in their technological aids, which, after much grumbling, they agreed to do.

Going back to basics, such as multiplication tables for the younger ones and algebra and geometry for the older ones, was a bit of a struggle but when they heard stories about how the Fanshaws lived back home on Earth, they started to take much more interest. The idea that there were machines that used oil and gas and other fossil fuels really surprised them, since they were all accustomed to using the power of the sun and, indeed, the very air round them as their main source of energy. The students also explained that everyone here had what was considered "normal powers" to use their own thoughts as tools for making things happen. They could move objects of any weight or size just by concentrating. If an object was really large, they would get two or three others who would all combine their thoughts to move the object. In addition, they often used telepathy to communicate with each other. They could even communicate with their robots.

Everyone wore what was known as "intelligent clothing," allowing for early diagnosis of any health or medical problems. A signal would go to a central medical centre and alert the doctors immediately should such a problem occur. Sometimes a cure could be delivered remotely, other times it would be necessary to go to a health centre, but it was very rare for anyone not to be cured or treated before the day ended. These people had long ago managed to cure cancer and diabetes and most other illnesses from which people on Earth suffered. Most people lived to at least 120 years old— some even longer—and they remained active and mentally aware up until the end. Of course when wars occurred, such as the most recent battle, casualties occurred, which was always sad. The Fanshaw family was fascinated by all this, and the children they taught were equally amazed at the Fanshaws' description of people and customs on Earth.

After the Fanshaws and children had shared stories of life on the two different planets, everyone felt that their lives had improved as a result. All seemed perfect, except that Walter began to wonder whether this was all real or just a dream. Everything seemed to be so perfect. The people around him appeared content, and there was no sign of danger as there had been before. Yet something was nagging him.

At that moment he began to feel a little strange. That odd tingling feeling that had happened back on Earth began to flow through his body again, and he felt himself spinning around faster and faster. Then he saw that his whole family was spinning with him, and that weird bubble that had taken them up into space was now encasing them, and with a mighty *whoosh!* it soared into the air. Again they experienced the amazing sight of the heavens rushing by with the myriads of stars and galaxies all around them. It was completely amazing and, even though it was slightly frightening,

they did not want it to end. However, all of a sudden it did, and with one huge *whoosh!* they came to a halt and found themselves back in their little house in Clapham. After a few shudders and shakes, the bubble evaporated and the Fanshaws were sitting round the same table as before.

It felt as if they had been away for an eternity, but then the most extraordinary thing happened: Walter just happened to look at the TV, which was showing the ten o clock news, and the news caster started the broadcast with the day's date. Incredibly, it was the same date they had left for the new world. In other words: time had stood still for them. Yet they had been in amazing battles and had experienced things that were almost beyond belief. Had it not been for the fact that all four of them had the same memory, it might have been some strange dream. Clearly that was not the case. It was hard to imagine how they would all return to their normal lives now. Indeed they were all pretty sure that this was just the beginning of many more adventures.

PART TWO

CHAPTER ONE
ANOTHER ADVENTURE

Walter Fanshaw and his family were now back in their own world after the most remarkable adventures. The trouble was that they could not tell anyone what had happened for the simple reason that nobody would believe them.

They also had a strong feeling that this was only the beginning of their new strange and inexplicable lives. All they could do was try to carry on as normally as possible and wait for the next event.

So Walter got up at his usual time the next morning and went off to the garage where he worked as a pump attendant and general handyman. Gertrude went to the supermarket and took up her position as a check out lady, and Rupert and Geraldine went off to school. For the next few days, life continued normally for all of them. After a while, they all began to wonder if they had experienced some kind of strange, collective dream or perhaps had eaten some mysterious food which made them all hallucinate.

On the seventh day after their adventure, while they were all sitting in the kitchen having their usual family supper, it suddenly started again. First the whole room seemed to change colours, switching from red to amber to green, just like traffic lights, and the air around them pulsated with a rhythmic sound of bells and drums. Then the revolving started and, once again, a great bubble began to slowly encase them. It glowed brightly and spun around, faster and faster, until it swept upwards and, as before, flew right through the ceiling and walls and up into the air. The bubble with the Fanshaws inside surged upwards into the stratosphere, hurtling through the stars and planets, all the while the Fanshaws sat transfixed in their chairs in a kind of trance.

Then with a gentle bump they found themselves back in the castle, and there, sitting on a huge wooden chair, was the strange character with the pointy ears and flashing eyes known as Cantrans. He was quite a small person actually and looked really odd in such a large chair. But he had a deep booming voice despite his size.

"Welcome back," he said. "I hope your journey was not too uncomfortable. I imagine you are asking yourselves why you are back again and whether this is some kind of dream."

Walter said, "Yes, we are still in shock from the last visit and cannot really understand what is happening to us."

Cantrans responded to this with what looked like a rather crooked smile and his eyes flashed even faster. "You proved yourselves to be exactly what we have been waiting for over many generations. In battle you were courageous and showed leadership and guidance. You showed how to guide our children in real learning, for which we are all truly thankful. But there is now a greater need for you." He then asked them to come outside with him. As they crossed over the great drawbridge, which was the access to the castle, he told them to look up at the sky, where they saw a strange sight. Two suns and two moons had appeared. On their last visit they had only seen one of each.

Walter expressed his surprise at this new situation.

"It is indeed very odd, but what we have discovered is that the second sun and the second moon are not the result of some change in the planets. Our scientists now know that these are artificial. Even though they have hardly moved in the sky since they arrived, we believe they are actually from some other world and may well be space ships of some kind. We have no idea whether they are friendly or hostile, but we fear the worst."

"So what can we possibly do to help?" asked Walter. "We have no knowledge of these things."

"No, but you have such great leadership abilities. We think that when the time comes we will need those very much," said Cantrans.

As they were standing looking at this strange sight, a huge flash of lightning filled the sky. It was followed by the most enormous roll of thunder that echoed around them and seemed to last forever. Walter and his family covered their ears from the sound and were extremely afraid. As the noise died away, they saw small objects come out of the newer sun and moon. As they drew nearer, it was clear that these objects were small spacecraft which soon filled the sky. Actually, they were very small indeed, no bigger than some of the small cars that Walter used to look after. The sky drew quite dark as it was filled with these objects. People came out of their homes and the castle to look up at the sky.

Everything became very still and quiet. Then all the little objects simply hovered two or three thousand feet above the land and began to shine with a kind of eerie green light.

Next a high-pitched sound emanated from above them and started to drill through the onlookers' heads. It was intense

and really quite unpleasant. The sound grew stronger and, as it did, some people started to scream with pain. When it seemed it was no longer bearable, it just stopped and all was quiet again.

Suddenly a pencil thin, white beam of light poured out of one of the objects onto one of the fields. As it reached the ground, a huge hole appeared where it touched down, and the beam simply continued drilling into the ground, creating a huge hole which seemed to disappear into the depths of the earth. The beam then disappeared as suddenly as it had appeared.

Now all was silent again. Everyone stood in amazement at these events with no idea what they meant and no idea what to do about them. Cantrans then asked Walter to come inside for a private chat. Once inside Cantrans said, "Walter, I did not want to frighten your family but I knew that some rather nasty people from another planet had plans to attack us, although I did not know exactly what they had in mind. As soon as I saw the new sun and moon, I realized that we would need help, which is why I have brought you here."

"But I have no idea what I can do," said Walter.

"Take a few moments to gather your thoughts. I am sure you will find a way," said Cantrans.

Walter sat alone for a few minutes and then called his family together. He explained the problem and the heavy burden that had been placed on his shoulders. Much to his surprise, they were all very positive and supportive.

"Come on, Dad," said Rupert, "old Cantrans would never have brought us here unless he was pretty convinced that we could help. Let's all have a good think and see what we come up with."

CHAPTER TWO
MEETING THE ALIENS

So the four sat there thinking, and while they did so a warm glow surrounded them, and their bubble friend started to envelope them. However, this time it did not sweep them up and take them home. No, it took them up into the air and, before they knew it, they found themselves inside one of the little space craft up in the sky. The space craft was tiny, but the amazing thing was that the four Fanshaws had been shrunk so that they easily could fit inside it.

Even stranger than that, however, was the fact that the Fanshaws were invisible to the occupants, who were indeed from another world. There were four of the aliens, and they were dressed in shimmering silk-like outfits. They had large heads, small bodies, and only one large finger on each hand. Their faces were blue and they had large flappy ears, a bit like an elephant, and rather pointed faces with a very pointy nose. They all had three eyes— two on each side and one in the middle. Despite the fact that they spoke a different language, Walter and his family could understand everything they said. Indeed, they even understood instructions being given from some central command.

Apparently this fleet of potential invaders from another planet had become endangered due to pollution and lack of water. They had been looking for a place where they could settle their people and, after many years searching for something that would suit them, they had discovered this one. Their technology was

extremely advanced, and they had many amazing skills but, in the process, they had nearly destroyed their environment.

On the one hand, Walter was sorry for their problems. Equally, however, he could not let them simply take over his new adopted home. It proved to be a real dilemma for him. He had watched his friends use their mind to transmit thoughts and move objects, even making them change shape. It was something he had tried to copy, but still was not skilled at doing. He knew that now was the time to use whatever powers he had to try to avoid what looked like a major disaster.

He concentrated as hard as he could and focused his attention on the alien who seemed to be the leader in this little craft. With all his powers of thought-control, he beamed a telepathic message to this creature requesting that they not be hostile or create havoc and destruction. It was a message of peace and a strong suggestion that talking would be better than waging war. As he beamed the message, the little cabin began to throb with a gentle blue light, bathing everyone in it, and a warm feeling washed over their bodies. It was obvious that the aliens were very affected. As the blue light moved slowly around the cabin, Walter could see that the other spacecraft also were beginning to glow with the same light. It was as though the whole sky was being painted with soft blue spots. The voices he had heard before became very calm and a message came into his mind: "We do not know who you are, but it is not our wish to destroy your world. We are looking for a new home. We need your help. Perhaps there is a way that we can live together in peace."

Walter was overjoyed at this response and beamed a message back: "Come to my castle down below and let my family and friends meet with your leaders to see how we can help you." At that moment he felt the bubble lift him away from the spacecraft and, within a few seconds, they were whisked back to the castle.

CHAPTER THREE
BACK IN THE CASTLE

As they entered the great hall, Walter was cheered by the locals, and they took up their positions at the head of the great long wooden table to await the arrival of the strange creatures.

After a short while, one of the walls opposite Walter began to shimmer and slowly turned into a huge screen like at a cinema. It shone brightly and four of the alien creatures appeared on the screen. They were dressed in multi-coloured robes. It was clear that the tallest of the four was the leader. As they watched this scene unfold, the creatures merely stepped out of the screen and slowly walked towards them. Walter welcomed them and beckoned to some helpers to provide chairs for the visitors. The discussions lasted for hours, as the aliens described in great detail what had happened to their planet.

First, many of their people had perished in horrendous floods and storms. Then the rains disappeared and searing heat parched the land causing cattle and crops to die. Part of this was caused by the huge pollution that had been created by industry. There also had been a small change in the position of their planet, which was caused by a tiny comet that had smashed into their orb, taking them closer to their sun and distorting the patterns of day and night. Over a period of fifty years, nearly three quarters of their population was destroyed. With their technology, they had been able to assemble a great armada of space vessels and had been seeking a new home for many years without too much success. Now they saw that Walter's planet, Lendorth, could offer them that refuge.

After hearing their story, the Council of Elders met in the big Chamber where all major decisions were made. It was resolved that these people should be welcomed and somehow they would find a place for them, even though they were very different. Of course there were some who were against this idea. They were worried that this could be a trick and once the aliens were given safe haven, they would seek to take over the planet for themselves. Others took the opposite view and thought that everyone should be able to live in peace, and maybe both sides could learn from each other with benefit to everyone.

One of the objectors, Strongband, was very loud in his opposition and, indeed, became very angry. His had always been a bit of an agitator and was not comfortable at the arrival of Walter and his family to his country, despite Walter's successes. "I am very concerned that these people will not fit well into our society. They look different from us and have different customs. We know nothing about them."

Walter explained about the many different races and cultures on his own planet. He said that over the years these different races and cultures had all been absorbed into one society. Although there had been clashes among those cultures from time to time, usually these had been resolved amicably. Now and then, of course, it had been difficult. Indeed in the Olden Days when his ancestors were fighting battles around the world, there had been major differences and, sadly, many people had died in the process. Gradually, however, people had learned to live together and share their different backgrounds. He strongly recommended that they give these people a chance to settle. The next question was how many of them were there and where would they go.

So Walter and his Council members, including the still rather seething Strongband, came back to their visitors and, with a warm smile, Walter explained that, despite some worries about their intentions, he was prepared to recommend that a place be found for them and everyone would do their best to help them to settle into their new homes. The aliens were absolutely delighted and showed their pleasure by puffing up their chests and twirling round and round while at the same time sending out little puffs of steam from their ears.

They told Walter that now there were only about 1,500 men, women and children in total. The rest had long since perished, either on their original planet or during the many years of searching the galaxies for a suitable new living place. They had many skilled people in a variety of talents amongst them, but they were not skilled not in everything so were happy to accept help from their new hosts.

After this conference, the alien leaders stepped back into the screen, which glowed for a few seconds before disappearing, leaving just the bare castle wall behind. Once they were gone, Strongband started shouting again and tried to get everyone to change their minds, but he did not succeed much to his annoyance.

"You will all live to regret this terrible mistake!" he growled.

CHAPTER FOUR
THE KATHUSIANS

Meanwhile the new visitors from the planet Kathus were in deep discussion. Strongband was not entirely wrong to think that there might be trouble ahead. The Kathusians had their own equivalent of Strongband, whose name was Brandarth. He was a tall version of their race and usually was able to get his way in an argument.

"These people look weak to me," Brandarth said, "and we could easily take over their world in five minutes with our superior technology, even though we are outnumbered many times. I think their planet looks very attractive. It's just what we have been searching for over these many years. I do not see any reason why we should share it with them. We are very different from them. Anyway, I think we are a much superior race."

He was a very good speaker and many nodded approval at this. However, their leader, who was older and in many ways wiser than Brandarth, took the floor.

"My friends, we have lost most of our population to the stupid ways adopted by our ancestors who poured polluting gases into our atmosphere and were constantly battling with each other over the diminishing resources of our previous home. We have been travelling through space for countless years and surely we must have learned something along the way. These people have welcomed us into their planet even though we are much different from them. We should take advantage of their kindness and try to find a way to live in peace. Maybe we are different, but that should not stop us from co-existing and doing our best to pass on our knowledge so that everyone can benefit. I strongly urge you all to take the path of peace. Let's at least give it a try and, over, time we will all discover more about each other."

After this, the people voted, with a large majority accepting the proposal. Brandarth and a few of his friends voted against the proposal, of course, but the majority won, and it was decreed that they would settle on Lendorth. A message was sent to Walter and his Council with this news. As with the Kathusians, it was necessary to let everyone on Lendorth vote on the idea, which was easily dealt with through electronic messages conveyed to each household. All they had to do was to think *Yes* or *No* and their thoughts were instantly translated into a vote. Again, some were anxious and unsure, so they voted against the measure, but the majority were in favour. Since they believed so much in Walter, and since he had recommended this idea, they were happy to follow.

The question was where to establish their new home. After discussion with some of Walter's people, it was decided that they should look at a place across the mountains about a day's march from the castle. Actually, the area was near the battle ground where Walter and his men had defeated their enemies some time ago. Although all was peaceful right now, it was recognized that everyone should be very careful.

Walter, riding his gleaming white horse, took a small group of heavily armed troops, all mounted on their hover boards and carrying multi-coloured banners. Riding alongside came the

Kathusians who, though much smaller, knew how to manage the hover boards and had their own secret weapons ready just in case. They crossed over the mountains and headed for the valley below. As they passed some villages, the people came out to watch in astonishment at this strange sight and then quickly withdrew into their huts.

The sky grew darker and, as had happened before, some very large, strange black birds swooped around their heads, making loud squawking noises. Some of the birds became especially daring and flew close to the tops of the troop's heads, looking as though they were going to scoop them up in their fearsome orange beaks. The Kathusians had a way of dealing with these birds. They sent out the same high-pitched whistling sound that Walter had heard before. From time to time, one Kathusian would simply point his finger at a bird and suddenly it would be frozen in ice and drop to the ground.

The troop camped that night in the middle of some woods and managed to get some sleep, despite the many odd sounds throughout the night.

The next morning the troop marched until they came upon a river flowing very fast in front of them. On the other side of the river lay the most beautiful green fields and flowers of every colour imaginable. In the sky above the fields was an even more amazing sight—a double rainbow. Walter had once heard of this phenomenon back on Earth, but had never actually seen one. It was sensational.

Then the Kathusians' mother spacecraft appeared above. It hovered over the countryside and slowly settled to the ground and

shone a bright light across the river. To their amazement, the river
parted in two, just like in the story of Moses and the parting of the
Red Sea from the old Bible stories that Walter had enjoyed as a boy.
Everyone quickly rushed across the parted river. No sooner were
they on the other side than the water came together again with

a great gurgling sound. Then the door of the spacecraft opened and out stepped more Kathusians looking very splendid in their shimmering uniforms. They greeted their colleagues and thanked Walter for bring them to this place.

"We will set up our homes here now and do our best to cause no harm," said their leader. "This is what we have been looking for many centuries, and we intend to avoid making the same mistakes that our ancestors made so many years ago. We were a little concerned about the people you defeated before. They looked a bit hostile to us and though we don't want to cause problems, it might be tricky in the future."

Walter understood their concerns and suggested that he might leave a few of his men to stay with them for a few days while they settled in. Obviously they needed to build houses and shelters very quickly, and his men would help with that. This was accepted and, after some fond farewells, Walter and his remaining men set off back home.

CHAPTER FIVE
THE CELEBRATION

Walter and his family were happy to have saved their adopted home from danger. He rather suspected that this was not the end of the story by a long stretch, but once again they celebrated with a great party to which some of the Kathusians who had stayed behind were invited. They had their own form of music and musical instruments, many of which seemed odd, including drums that played themselves and some weird form of bagpipes that actually were made with real live snakes. They also fixed some strong drinks that made everyone a bit dizzy, but had assured were harmless. And, unlike those that created an enormous hangover the next morning, these drinks had the opposite effect and would actually make you feel happy and energetic the next day.

The next morning Walter and his family started to feel that familiar sensation which they now knew was a signal that they were to return home. They gathered together and the bubble enveloped them with its usual pulsating beat. Soon they were hurtling back home and, once again, found themselves in the cosy kitchen in Clapham.

As always, Walter knew there would be more journeys to come. He also knew that, even though he had left a peaceful world with people intent on living happily together, it was entirely possible there could be trouble ahead. But for the moment, members of the Fanshaw family were back in their normal routines and, as always, it was impossible to tell any of their friends about what was happening to them.

Walter carried on at the garage and his wife at the supermarket while the children were, as usual, back at school. In addition, as before, it seemed that time had stood still while they were away—in fact, no one even noticed that they had been away. The only odd thing was that people noticed their eyes had changed colour— the Fanshaws all now had green eyes instead of the rather bluey grey colour from before. None of the Fanshaws could explain this to anyone. And it was not just that they were green, they were bright flashy emerald green!

Walter's boss at the garage suggested he go see the optician, but Walter simply responded that this must be a throwback to the ancient days of his ancestors, who were known to have that colour of eyes. It seemed to satisfy his boss, even though Walter knew that the real truth was very different.

Gertrude's boss did not even notice the change, but one of her regular customers at the checkout made a comment. She simply looked at Gertrude and, as their eyes met, both sets started to flash and both were emerald green.

"Have a nice day," said the customer with a slightly crooked smile and went on her way.

Review Requested:
If you loved this book, would you please provide a
review at Amazon.com?

Thank You

Lightning Source UK Ltd.
Milton Keynes UK
UKOW02f0806281016

286278UK00001BB/37/P